GEO

P9-CND-500

10 Things You Need to Know About

Becoming a Pop Star

by Jen Jones

Capstone press®

Mankato, Minnesota

Snap Books are published by Capstone Press,
151 Good Counsel Drive, P.O. Box 669, Mankato, Minnesota 56002.
www.capstonepress.com

Library of Congress Cataloging-in-Publication Data
Jones, Jen.
    Becoming a pop star / by Jen Jones.
    p. cm. — (Snap books. 10 things you need to know about)
    Summary: "Provides information on the skills needed to become a pop star, including songwriting,
dancing, touring, and dealing with fame" — Provided by publisher.
    Includes bibliographical references and index.
    ISBN-13: 978-1-4296-1342-2 (hardcover)
    ISBN-10: 1-4296-1342-4 (hardcover)
    1. Popular music — Vocational guidance — Juvenile literature. I. Title. II. Series.
ML3928.J66 2008
781.64023 — dc22   2007028285

Editors: Kathryn Clay and Christine Peterson
Designer and Illustrator: Juliette Peters
Photo Researchers: Charlene Deyle and Jo Miller
Photo Stylist: Kelly Garvin

Photo Credits:
AP Images/Kevork Djansezian, 14;
Capstone Press/Karon Dubke, cover, 4, 7, 8, 11 (left), 12, 13 (left), 15, 18, 20, 21, 24, 26, 27, 30
Corbis/Creasource, 5
Getty Images Inc./Dave M. Benett, 11 (right); Frank Micelotta, 19; Michelle Cop, 22; Peter Kramer, 25 (right)
Michele Torma Lee, 32
Shutterstock/Adam Gasson, 9; Adam J. Sablich, 13 (right); Candice M. Cunningham, 25 (left)
ZUMA Press/Mike Valdez, 16–17

Capstone Press thanks Two Fish Studios in Mankato, Minn., for assisting with photo shoots for this book.

1 2 3 4 5 6 13 12 11 10 09 08

Table of Contents

Introduction

In the '60s, teens went crazy for the Beatles. In the '90s, fans flipped over the Backstreet Boys. Today, props are given to pop stars like Beyoncé and Justin Timberlake. Pop music has proven its popularity over the years, and it's here to stay. Tons of talented acts are hoping for their big break. This book will help you tap into your own talents. You'll find out how to reach the top of the charts. Take a break from practicing your moves in the mirror, and let's get loud!

Getting a head start

Have you been rockin' the mike since you were a tyke? If so, you could have the makings of a great pop star. Many of today's music superstars began singing at a young age. Destiny's Child got its start in Beyoncé Knowles' backyard. Back then, the group was called Girls' Tyme, and Beyoncé was just 8 years old. Before hitting it big, the group competed on the talent program *Star Search*. They also sang at local events.

Many pop hopefuls get some great singing experience in their hometowns. You can too. Singing in the school choir or taking voice lessons can teach you a lot. Check out other opportunities to shine in community dance or theater groups. Soon you'll be primed to go from the backyard to the big time.

In the Mouse House: *The New Mickey Mouse Club*

Many of the Mouseketeers from the popular '90s Disney Channel show are today's pop stars. Stars like Britney Spears, Christina Aguilera, and JC Chasez and Justin Timberlake of *NSYNC got their big break on *The New Mickey Mouse Club*. (Jessica Simpson tried out but didn't make the cut!)

2 Image is everything

To make it to the top, a strong voice is a must. Yet singing skills don't always lead to success. Today, a pop star must have the total package. Looks, talent, and personality all come into play when building star power. Blending into the crowd is not an option.

Think about your favorite pop stars. Most singers have a look that fits their music and personality. Creating a unique image can make or break a pop star's success. Punk princess Avril Lavigne burst onto the scene with her trademark look of cool men's ties and tank tops. Singer Pink made a splash with her spiky hot pink hairdo. This bold move set off her edgy pop/rock music. By setting themselves apart with style, pop stars become instantly unforgettable.

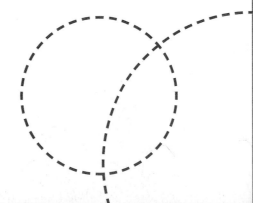

Pink

Rising to the top is often a family affair

When accepting awards, pop stars often thank their family members. It's no wonder they appreciate their families so much. After all, it takes a major support system to travel the road to stardom. Parents pay big bucks for singing lessons, clothing, and professional pics for their young stars. For many pop hopefuls, a change of address is a must. Some families move to Hollywood or New York City to try to boost their child's career.

Young pop stars often keep it all in the family by hiring their parents as managers. Managers guide pop stars' careers and handle their schedules. This lets the family keep track of a star's money and image. But too much togetherness isn't always a good thing. Even worse, pop stars might feel like their parents treat them like employees rather than family members. It's a tricky balance between business and family.

3 1833 05416 2356

Family Matters

Wondering which famous singers have their families working for them? Check this out:

❀ Joe Simpson manages the careers of both his famous daughters, Jessica and Ashlee Simpson. Their mom, Tina, acts as the stylist for these successful sisters.

❀ Beyoncé Knowles is managed by her dad, Matthew. Her mom, Tina, designs her costumes.

❀ Dina Lohan manages her daughter, actress and pop star Lindsay Lohan.

4 Poets make great songwriters

Are you a whiz with words? If so, you might make a great songwriter. Catchy hooks and relatable lyrics are the name of the game. Performers earn more respect if they can write and perform music.

If you're trying to top the music charts and have writer's block, there's no need to worry. There are plenty of ways to dream up future hits.

✤ Pick a title, and then go from there. Take moments from your life and put them to music. A day with friends could turn into "Girls' Day Out." Jot down words that go along with your title.

✤ Listen to some of your favorite songs. How are they put together? What lyrics and melodies stand out to you?

✤ Playing an instrument is a great starting point. Try different melodies to see what catches your ear. Then pair up words with your tune.

Honor Roll

These talented singer/songwriters all scored top 10 singles on the Billboard charts with songs they wrote:

🌸 John Mayer — "Waiting on the World to Change"

🌸 Nelly Furtado — "Say it Right"

🌸 Kelly Clarkson — "Because of You"

Nelly Furtado

5 All the right moves

When Usher does his signature moves on stage, crowds go wild. Same goes for Shakira shaking her hips. For pop stars, singing and dancing go together. A hot dance beat can make all the difference for a new song. If a song fills the dance floor, you know it's a hit.

To do their songs justice, pop stars must be able to bust a move. Many stars work with choreographers to polish their dance skills and prepare for performances. You can perfect your own dance moves by taking lessons at a local studio.

Pop stars get to show off their stuff at live shows. Artists like Justin Timberlake, Jennifer Lopez, and Janet Jackson are known for their fancy footwork and flashy dance numbers.

Justin Timberlake

Creating an instant star

With the push of a telephone button, a pop star is born. Millions of voters have helped crown American Idols like Kelly Clarkson and Carrie Underwood. The hugely popular show has become a star-making machine. In 2006, Clarkson was named "Favorite Pop/Rock Female Artist" at the American Music Awards. Underwood went on to make the fastest-selling country album of all time. She has hits on the pop charts as well.

As the show's popularity has grown, so has the number of Idol hopefuls. Each season, thousands of people flock to major cities to try out for the show. People tune in to see the talented few who are trying to make their mark in the pop music world.

Takin' it back to the old school

American Idol is far from a new idea. TV talent shows have been on the air for years. *Showtime at the Apollo* helped start the careers of pop stars Michael Jackson and Lauryn Hill. Singing group Eden's Crush was formed on the TV show *Popstars*.

Star Search was another stage to success. The original show ran from 1983 to 1995. Performers competed in several different categories. Alanis Morrissette and Christina Aguilera sang on this show.

7 Pop stars have strength in numbers

Are you willing to share the spotlight? If so, a pop group could be your perfect path to fame. Being part of a group lets you experience the ups and downs of pop life with friends by your side. Wherever pop groups go, fan frenzy follows. From look-alike dolls to T-shirts and magazine covers, a successful pop group becomes all the rage.

Members of pop groups must get along. After all, they spend countless hours together practicing, touring, and recording. Each person must have skills that work well in the group. Some group members play instruments, while others may write songs.

Sometimes the lead singer of a group becomes a breakout star and leaves the group to try it alone. Beyoncé's stardom started with Destiny's Child. Justin Timberlake once rocked the mike with *NSYNC. Both singers now enjoy huge solo success, but they'll never forget the groups that started it all.

Destiny's Child

Young singers often make demo tapes. These recordings show off a singer's skills. Most singers record three or four songs for the demo. They sing original tunes and those made famous by other stars. For singer/songwriters, it's important to use their own songs. That way, listeners get a sense of the singer's style.

Recording a demo takes a lot of time and money. Renting a recording studio can cost $300 to $500 per day, plus other fees. To cut costs, many studios offer package deals that include studio time, sound mixing, the final recording, and CDs. Some singers save cash by recording at home, although the quality is not as good.

Once a demo is ready, the singer shops it around to radio stations and record companies. If record executives like what they hear, the singer just might get a recording contract. Some lucky pop hopefuls get their song on a radio station's playlist. Artists also create MySpace pages to get their music out to the public.

9 Be prepared to hit the road

Guy Sebastian

Every rising pop star dreams of selling out a huge arena. But without a fan base, those arena seats could stay empty. To get the word out about their music, new pop stars often go on small, local tours. Before Britney Spears hit it big, she did a mall tour where people could hear her perform for free. Britney was able to reach more people and grab their attention. Several albums later, it looks like that tour was a pretty good move.

The American music market can be tough for unknown singers. Some singers decide to take their shows to other countries first. This gives singers a chance to prove their talent and win fans. If singers impress audiences in Europe or Asia, they might become opening acts on major U.S. concert tours. It's all part of the ladder to success as a pop star.

10 Pop stars shine in the media spotlight

Today's pop stars spend much of their time in the media spotlight. Their faces are splashed on the covers of teen magazines. Pop stars perform live and in videos shown on music television. They also spend a lot of time promoting their CDs. Stars may spend the day chatting with a reporter from *Rolling Stone* or appearing on *Saturday Night Live*. They might wake up early to do a call-in show for a radio station. With a new CD to promote, a pop star is on the go 24/7.

Awards shows also help pop stars get noticed. At red carpet events like the Video Music Awards or the Grammys, stars pose for pictures and talk with reporters.

Of course, media coverage never stops when you're a pop star. Even when stars are just having lunch or running errands, they can expect to have their pictures taken. It's a glamorous life, but it's lived under a microscope.

Jessica Simpson

Gimme an M!
Gimme a T!
Gimme a V!

In 2011, MTV will turn 30 years old. Yet the famed cable channel is far from over the hill. MTV keeps up with the trends of its young viewers. The channel has played a major role in the rise of pop acts ranging from Blink-182 to the Black Eyed Peas.

A Few More Things You Need to Know

Pop stars love to change their images

To stand the test of time, a pop star must be willing to change with the trends. Madonna is a star with staying power. From the '80s lady in lace to today's pop queen, Madonna's changing image has kept her in the public eye. Maybe that's why the *Guinness Book of World Records* named her the highest paid female singer on earth.

Singers often cross over to the pop world

In today's music market, a song that tops the specialty charts often crosses over to the pop charts. As the lines between music styles blur, pop stars move over to make room for everyone from country singers to Latino legends. Shania Twain and Shakira are two singers who hit it big with their own styles before topping the pop charts.

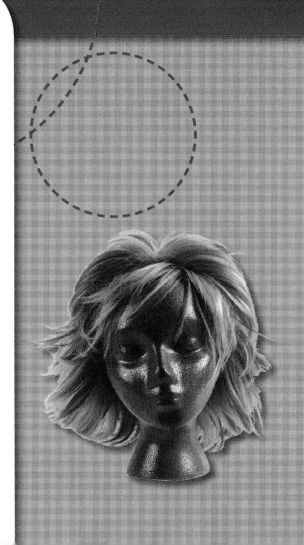

One-hit wonders have a sentimental place in history

When pop stars have a monster hit, the press and the public often have high hopes for their future songs. Yet sometimes the pop act fizzles out as soon as their song drops off the charts. These groups and singers join the long list of pop music's one-hit wonders. (Yes, Vanilla Ice, we're talking about you.)

Being a "triple threat" triples your chances

Can you sing, dance, and act? If so, you're what the industry calls a "triple threat." Having many skills opens the door to just about any job. In musicals, pop stars get a chance to show off all their talents at once. Beyoncé did just that in the film *Dreamgirls*, and Usher lit up Broadway in the musical *Chicago*.

Your friends nominate you to be first up at karaoke. What do you do?
- A Cringe and hide under the table
- B Recruit a few friends to sing along with you
- C Belt out a tune that has the crowd begging for more

Which *American Idol* judge would you most want to have lunch with?
- A Paula Abdul
- B Randy Jackson
- C Simon Cowell

What item do you never leave home without?
- A Your journal
- B Your cell phone
- C Your iPod

When you're the center of attention, what do you do?
- A Shift the attention to someone else
- B Make a joke, then change the subject
- C Enjoy every second in the spotlight

If you could live anywhere, you would live in:
- A Chicago
- B New York
- C Los Angeles

For Christmas, you ask for:
- A A subscription to *Cosmo! Girl*
- B Tickets to go see *Total Request Live*
- C Voice lessons

It's picture day at school. What are you thinking?
- A "Can I call in sick?"
- B "These things never turn out right!"
- C "I can't wait to show off the pose I've been practicing for weeks!"

You take a trip to Hollywood. What's the first thing you do?
A Take the Star Homes Tour
B Go take a picture by the Hollywood sign
C Invade the nearest casting office

Someone gives you a gift certificate to the nearest dance studio. What class do you sign up for?
A Ballet
B Jazz
C Hip-hop

What annoying habit do you have?
A Biting your nails
B Talking too loud
C Singing in the shower

In the talent show at school, what act do you perform?
A A skit with friends
B An upbeat dance number
C A solo rendition of a Christina Aguilera tune

What's your favorite video game?
A Guitar Hero
B Dance Dance Revolution
C Karaoke Revolution

How much bling do you own?
A I prefer to wear simple jewelry.
B I've got some ice, baby.
C Prepare to be blinded if you open my jewelry chest.

What's your favorite MTV reality show?
A *The Real World*
B *The Hills*
C *Making the Band*

Who's your Hollywood crush?
A Daniel Radcliffe
B Jesse McCartney
C Justin Timberlake

When scoring your answers, A equals 5 points, B equals 3 points, and C equals 1 point. Total them up and find out your Hollywood destiny!

1-25 = Christina and Shakira better watch out, because your star is on the rise!

26-50 = You've got the confidence and style to make it as a pop star. Turn it up a notch, and you'll skyrocket to stardom.

51-75 = You've got pop star potential, but it's hidden under your protective shell. Come out, come out, wherever you are!

Glossary

choreographer (kor-ee-OG-ruh-fur) — someone who creates and arranges dance steps

demo (DEM-oh) — a recording made to show off a new performer or piece of music

lyrics (LIHR-iks) — the words of a song

playlist (PLAY-list) — a list of songs radio station play during a certain program or time of day

promote (pruh-MOTE) — to make the public aware of something or someone

unique (yoo-NEEK) — one of a kind

Read More

Jones, Jen. *Being Famous.* 10 Things You Need to Know About. Mankato, Minn.: Capstone Press, 2008.

Orme, David. *How to Be a Pop Star.* Trailblazers. United Kingdom: Ransom, 2006.

Schaefer, A.R. *Making a First Recording.* Rock Music Library. Mankato, Minn.: Capstone Press, 2004.

Tauber, Michelle. *Make Me a Pop Star.* New York: Little, Brown, 2005.

Internet Sites

FactHound offers a safe, fun way to find Internet sites related to this book. All of the sites on FactHound have been researched by our staff.

Here's how:

1. Visit *www.facthound.com*
2. Choose your grade level.
3. Type in this book ID **1429613424** for age-appropriate sites. You may also browse subjects by clicking on letters, or by clicking on pictures and words.
4. Click on the **Fetch It** button.

FactHound will fetch the best sites for you!

About the Author

Though she can't sing a tune to save her life, Jen Jones will always be a teenybopper at heart. A freelance writer based in Los Angeles, Jones has written for magazines such as *American Cheerleader*, *Dance Spirit*, *Ohio Today*, and *Pilates Style*. Her work has also appeared on *E! Online* and *PBS Kids*, and Web sites for shows like *The Jenny Jones Show*, *The Sharon Osbourne Show*, and *The Larry Elder Show*. She has also written books on gymnastics and fashion for young girls.

Index